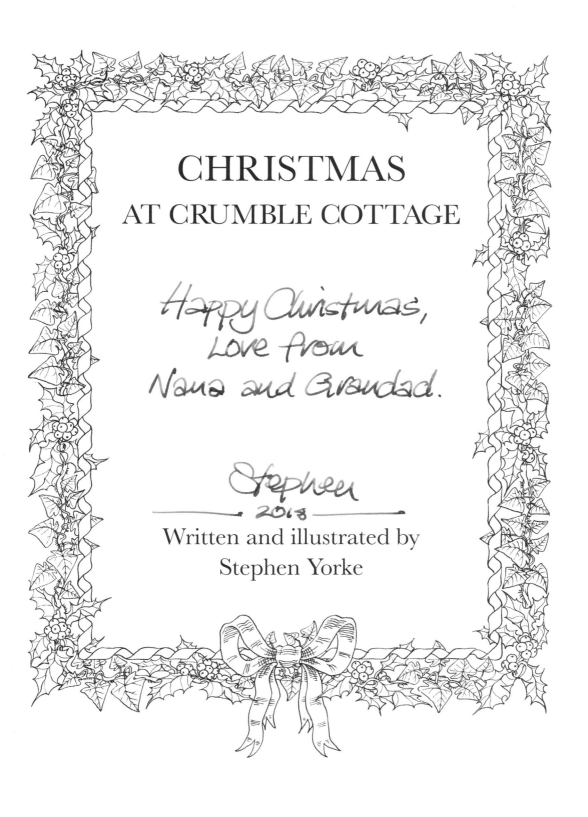

CHRISTMAS
AT CRUMBLE COTTAGE

Happy Christmas,
Love from
Nana and Grandad.

Stephen
2018

Written and illustrated by
Stephen Yorke

ISBN: 978-0-9573730-0-6

Typeset in Baskerville by Backtofrontdesign.

Printed and bound in England
by The Printing House UK

Crumble Cottage Ltd.
Palladium House
1-4 Argyll Street
London
W1F 7LD

For Christmas-lovers everywhere
Whose joy it is to give, to share.

This then, for children of all ages
To take delight between these pages.

TO CHRISTMAS LOVERS
EVERYWHERE

osemary and her husband Sedgewick lived at Crumble Cottage, Upper Crustington, Breadfordshire, next to the bakery, which was convenient as he was the village baker. They both shared three passions, baking, each other and Christmas. Rosemary had caught it from her grandmother at a very early age. A fever and fervour, which quickly spread to those around her and to her husband when they were newly-wed. The symptoms, which were perennial, would begin to show in the early autumn around St Michaelmas Day and included a heightened excitement lasting through to the end of Advent. This inherited, highly-infectious love of Christmas also produced a deep adhesion to tradition, which came with quaint side-effects of superstitions – some bordering on the ridiculous. Here then, is a collection of recollections of Rosemary and Sedgewick – two people who love, and live for, Christmas.

MAGICAL MINCE PIES

nce upon a time, exactly a quarter past six on the morning of December 21st in fact, Rosemary began making her mince pies. Her husband, Sedgewick, was the village baker and, having already baked his bread, the oven was perfectly hot. On this Midwinter's Day she would be making six hundred of her meltingly-crumbly mince pies. The day, being the shortest of the year, would nevertheless offer most of itself to her loving task. The mincemeat she had made herself on St Michaelmas Day, and had been maturing in the cellar ever since. The pastry dough – a whispered secret – she made in batches, each left to chill and rest in the scullery until called upon to receive her rolling pin and her light, magical touch. All her friends awaited delivery of her pies, and who wouldn't? Because as we all know, Christmas isn't Christmas without a magical mince pie.

A CHRISTMAS CAROL

heir enthusiasm and determination no-one could doubt and no-one ever did. Even though it was rather late and more than a few of the villagers of Upper Crustington were more than contemplating going to bed. The fault was falsetto. If he stayed within his range, Sedgewick was a passable tenor. But, much to the choir-master's frustration, he was prone to drift perilously upwards – never quite making the ascent. Yet inspite of this and the hour, Rosemary and he, returning from practice for the forthcoming Christmas Carol Concert, couldn't help stopping in the street to give "Oh, come all ye faithful", another try. Yet far from trying the villagers' patience, their doors and windows would be flung open and their neighbours would join in the chorus and applaud when they had finished. All truly faithful friends indeed.

BRINGING HOME
THE TREE

osemary seldom went to the Great Wood in winter. One of the exceptions being one day, the 22nd December, when she and Sedgewick would go and find their Christmas tree. He insisted on her help in choosing the perfect specimen, though she knew it was more to do with helping him push the cart up the hill to the wood. There, in a secret corner, they chose from their own little plantation of fir trees. They expanded this every year, due to the fact that, for every tree they cut down, they planted two new ones. She would then select huge bunches of holly and of mistletoe, While Sedgewick would wield his axe. Her final task was to ride on the cart and apply the hand brake on the bumpy, downward, homeward slope. And to remember to duck under the overhanging branches of the trees – ouch!

14

DRESSING THE TREE

t was the evening of 22nd of December and of all the many, many things Rosemary loved about Christmas, this was amongst her favourites. It wasn't just the fact that she and her husband had grown it themselves, cut it themselves or how proud it stood dressed in it's tartan bows and shimmering candles, which by themselves, lit the room in a sublime glow. Nor was it the beautiful aroma of fresh pine it emitted throughout the house. No, though she loved her garlands and wreaths, it was at this precise, magical moment, as Sedgewick lit the last of the candles and she placed the presents beneath, that for her, the spirit of Christmas had truly arrived at Crumble Cottage. And as they both stood back to toast their work with a glass of dry sherry, the spirit had arrived in more ways than one!

THE MULL BEFORE
THE STORM

edgewick had rushed back to Crumble Cottage after performing in the Christmas Carol Concert. Time was short. He had the woodstove fire to light, oranges to slice and bottles to uncork. As with all obsessions, his mulled wine preparations were methodical. The red wine warmed gently in the pan as he added exact quantities of cloves, cinnamon, star anise, raw cane sugar and, lastly, the orange slices. His stirring wafted the unmistakeable aroma of Christmas up the cellar stairs and into the house where the rest of the choir had congregated to congratulate one another on their success over his mulled wine and his wife's mince pies. With Rosemary performing waitress duties, he ladled his second glass in order, he told himself, to determine if the spice blend was just right. From the increasing hubbub emanating from upstairs, his fellow choristers seemed to agree that it was.

HANGING THE WREATH

osemary started, as her grandmother had taught her, with a skeleton circle of willow canes onto which, she wired a thick bed of moss. Then came the laurel leaves and sprigs of mistletoe, all beautifully and carefully arranged until all the moss was covered. When she was finally satisfied, she added the white satin ribbon, which she tied in two beautiful bows – one at the top, the other at the bottom. The hard part done, next came the simple task of hanging the Christmas wreath on the front door of Crumble Cottage. Rosemary and Sedgewick had performed this task each Christmas for countless years. Which made it all the more odd that he hadn't yet learnt that wearing hob-nail boots, climbing three-legged milking stools balanced on icy doorsteps are not the safest combination. Fortunately for him, the wreath hung undamaged – rather like his head as he limped indoors.

GRATE EXPECTATIONS

t was Christmas Eve. The air and the fire crackled with anticipation, the mince pies and glass of port wine left on the hearth – a reviving snack for Saint Nicholas. Each year, Rosemary and Sedgewick would hang their stockings on the mantelshelf. This year, however, he couldn't help noticing the prodigious size of his wife's stocking. A shocking stocking. Inwardly, he smiled. Was she playing one of her tricks to tease him? Or had she guessed that he had been overtly generous with his choice of gifts for her? It was a mystery. Rather like the fact that neither of them knew how or when the other chanced to fill their partner's stocking. They never spoke of it. Well not everything can be explained can it? And after all, a little Christmas mystery is in itself rather like a gift left tantalisingly unopened.

CHRISTMAS SPIRIT

t was mid-morning on Christmas Eve and Sedgewick was making his final delivery before Christmas. In typical seasonal festive cheer, he had given his usual delivery boy the day off. He cycled up Church Lane to the cottages that bordered the churchyard, whistling "The Holly and the Ivy", when suddenly something else whistled past his ear. From nowhere a volley-fire of snowballs, one of which hit him square on the nose, sending him, bread and bicycle together tumbling into the snow! The youngsters, realizing their mistake, rushed to help him, gathering his loaves and righting his bicycle. " We're very sorry, Mr Sedgewick, Sir. We expected to see your lad," they chorused. "We'll deliver those for you and a Merry Christmas, Sir." Sedgewick, whose festive spirit had briefly given up the ghost, accepted their apology and their offer. After all, he'd been a youngster once too.

THE YULE LOG

he Yule Log, as tradition would have it, must be hewn from a windfall tree and not one felled by hand. The wood is to be burnt in the Christmas Eve hearth. To this end, Sedgewick always wandered in The Great Wood on the last Sunday before Christmas (being a baker's day off) in search of an old oak tree. In spite of the deep snow, he had found his fallen hero and was chopping merrily away. Meanwhile, in the warm heart of the Crumble Cottage kitchen, Rosemary had just retrieved her chocolate sponge from the oven and was leaving it to cool, whipping her cream to soft peaks. Then, after searching the shelves and her beloved walnuts found, she too was chopping merrily away. She had only just iced the log and placed the holly and ivy decoration, when the kitchen door opened and each simultaneously presented their morning's labours.

A DOWNHILL DOWNFALL

e had been Village Sledding Champion eight times, the last being some fifteen years ago. Or was it sixteen? Never mind, Sedgewick sat astride his trusty (slightly rusty) charger. High above the village and in high spirits, he pushed off. As he waved to the gathered throng at the church gate he had a feeling he shouldn't be there. He was right. The course turned to the left before the church and now there was no way out. At break-neck and brake-less speed he plunged into the High Street, veering to miss the stone cross in the square and spraying Rosemary and villagers alike with snow and ice. Fate and the sledge took a turn and his new course sent him clattering across the frozen duck pond and into the sedge (appropriately) and snow on the far bank. He had broken two things. The race rules and his shattered old friend.

UNFORGETTABLE CHRISTMAS PUDDINGS

 osemary was a stout lady. That is to say she always preferred the dark, velvety liquid in her mixture above any other beverage. It was the first Sunday in Advent – the day she made her Christmas puddings. Not a day earlier or a day later. A mild crisis unveiled itself on her discovering that Sedgewick had forgotten to buy the bottled beer again! In fairness, he readily admitted his guilt and donned his coat, scarf and hat and plunged forth into the dark afternoon to throw himself on the mercy of the local hostelry. She knew he would return in an hour carrying four pints of ale, but only two of them in bottles. She mixed the dry ingredients in readiness and cut the muslin cloth in which the puddings would steam. "It's the same every year," she warmly whispered to the cat and silently smiled to herself.

MISTLETOE TO TOE

osemary was very particular about selecting her mistletoe. As with many Christmas traditions, superstition surrounded the mythic, parasitic plant. It had to be mistletoe growing on an oak tree, as this was the rarest. It couldn't be allowed into the house before Christmas Eve and must be gone by the end of Advent. Once all of these criteria were fulfilled, she delighted in hanging several sprays around the house repeating a rhyme each time. It was a song her grandparents had repeatedly sung and lovingly danced together in this same room when she was very young.

"Seek your bough on secret Oak
In deepest wood in grove unspoke
Your hall be-deck with mythic sprig
Start the fiddle, play a jig."

"Gentle Sir, take your Miss
And take a berry with each kiss
It's magic sets lovers' hearts aglow
Under mistletoe to toe."

PATIENCE IS A VIRTUE

osemary had baked her dark, dense fruit cake a week ago and enrobed it in marzipan. In order to allow the oil in the almond paste to dry out and therefore not stain the icing, it would need to rest for seven long days. Sedgewick, however, would not rest. He had asked her every day when the cake would be ready. So today was Royal Icing Day and she banished him from the kitchen until it was finished. The smooth, even, snow-white coating needed a steady hand and a calm atmosphere. Even more so when she piped her snowballs and added exquisite holly leaves and berries to the top. "It still needs twenty four hours to dry," she told Sedgewick, whose now crestfallen head he had poked round the kitchen door. She laughed, placing a second cake on the table and said, "But here's one I made earlier!"

IN FOR A ROASTING

t had been snowing continuously throughout the day of their mince-pie-manufacturing marathon and was still silently falling as they settled themselves by the warm hearth. On such a bitterly-cold night as this, Rosemary wouldn't hear of Sedgewick venturing out to deliver her pies – that could easily wait until the morning. And besides it was time to sample this year's harvest of their sweet chestnuts. As she poured them both a glass of her own Damson Gin, Sedgewick loaded his special, lidded pan and bathed it in the flames, taking great care not to allow the centres to turn to charcoal! Eagerness got the better of prudence and almost burning his fingers, he pealed the first two, handing one to his wife. "The first of many," thought Rosemary as she savoured the roasted kernel. Still chewing, they took a sip and simultaneously proclaimed, "They are as sweet as…well, a nut!"

THE LOG STORE

THE LOG STORE

edgewick was fond of his log store, if not a little territorial too. When Rosemary teased him about it, he quickly defended his careful stacking (oak and beech separate from apple and pear wood, for instance), his grading in size of the kindling sticks and even the importance of log rotation. In fairness, the wood was not just for the house fires, he used it in his bread oven too and, as some woods burn hotter than others, it was all about the temperature. He nevertheless spent more time in there than he needed to, but he loved the smell of freshly-split logs as much as his newly-baked bread. He did, however, share his domain with a family of robins who had returned to nest and roost year after year. They knew all too well that where there's a baker, there are always breadcrumbs!

CHANCING ON ICE

It was Boxing Day morning some years ago. The air was crisp and clear. Already, the more enthusiastic were carving their sweeping patterns across the frozen millpond. Rosemary had started, as she did every year, to plead against Sedgewick participating in what she felt, a reckless pursuit. She continued, her voice ascending, as they descended the lane and concluded, at the very edge of the pond, in reminding her husband of his increasing years! Without doubt, he was miffed! With over-exuberance he sniffed and of more than a little hubris he whiffed. Fortunately, eager helping hands were on hand to pull him from the icy water and within ten minutes he was steaming in front of the kitchen fire in Crumble Cottage with an equally steaming glass of mulled-wine in his cupped hands. The skates were hung in the cellar – unspoken of and untouched to this day.

A CHRISTMAS CLANGOUR

It was very early in the morning on Christmas Day when Sedgewick was woken by the bell ringing. It was the doorbell and grave news indeed. Old Heythrop, one of the bell-ringers, was bed-ridden with fever and there was no-one to pull the tenor. It had been many years since he had handled a Sally, but with the Christmas Peal being such a proud tradition in the village, he found himself, with some trepidation, in the ringing-chamber of the belfry. The ring-leader called, "Gone," and marked the start of their Grandsire Triples. Sedgewick, his face taught with concentration, had kept time and pace until he forgot one thing – to let go of his Sally. Heading Heaven-wards, and snagging his neighbour's rope, caused what should have been, "Tin tan, din dan, bim bam, bom bo," to descend into, "Tin tangle, din dangle, bing bang, bom bomb." Oh, my dear Lord!

ROSEMARY'S MOMENT

t had been snowing heavily throughout the night and now through the window she saw how it lay crisp and even. It was five and twenty past two in the afternoon of Christmas Day and the low winter sun was shining, it's rays bouncing off the pure, white snow and up-lighting the room in that rare, curious fashion. Rosemary had been up since half past six, busy with preparations and dizzy with excitement. For her, this was a magical moment, the culmination of weeks of loving effort and months of feverish anticipation. This was the Christmas dinner. Those near and dear to herself and Sedgewick had gathered around the table, all very jolly and jolly eager. Her goose was cooked (and so was the leg of pork) beautifully and accompanied by all the traditional tasty trimmings. They all raised their glasses and chorused, "A Merry Christmas, everyone!"

A CHRISTMAS TOAST

he fire crackled brightly, the clock chimed softly and Sedgewick snored loudly. "A case of body filled and mind vacant," Rosemary thought, as she watched him and smiled. The glow of the fire couldn't match the glow in her heart. It had been a truly memorable Christmas dinner – a full three hours long and every minute golden to her. Even Great Aunt Augusta, who was prone to offer culinary critiques, had commented favourably on her stuffing, which was a first. Although she had found the goose "delicious," but the pork "bland," which was odd, as she hadn't been served any pork! The afternoon's laughter, the chattering and the clattering of cutlery still echoed in her ears making her chuckle to herself. She raised her sherry glass and wriggled her toes on her footstool giving them and herself, a well-earned Christmas toast.

And so, from Sedgewick and Rosemary,
Who wish your Christmas merry
Full of love, laughter and cheer
And bid you all a happy New Year.